THE MARLIN

MADELINE SUNSHINE

For Steven

Cover Illustration by Elizabeth Koda-Callan

Illustrations by Leland Neff

ISBN 0-590-35214-8

12 11 10 9 8 7 6 5 4

1 2/9
31

CHAPTER 1

The chase was on. Ricky held tightly to the wheel of his boat. He turned the wheel hard to the left. Water sprayed the air. He looked behind him. The other boat was getting close, but Ricky wasn't worried, at least not yet. He knew these waters like the back of his hand. He thought back to his first day on the Marlin. He remembered Captain Pulaski saying: "A good captain has to know how to read the waters."

"Read the waters? What do you mean?" Ricky had asked him.

"Reading the ocean," the captain had said, "is like reading a book. But, instead of words, the story is told in colors. Clear blue means deep water, green means shallow water, and brown means reefs."

Back then, Ricky hadn't known what reefs were. But he knew now. They were underwater rocks — rocks big enough to wreck any boat that hit them.

Ricky looked up at the sky. It was getting dark fast. That wasn't a good sign. Just then Ricky heard the roar of an engine behind him. The other boat was almost on top of him!

"I've got to do something!" said Ricky, but there was no one to hear him. He was all alone.

He turned back to the wheel. He knew he had to go faster. It was his only chance.

Just then he spotted something. He let out a low whistle. There was brown water up ahead.

Now he had a plan. Maybe the other boat's captain hadn't spotted the reefs yet.

"Wahoo!" he shouted. "I'm home free!"

The Marlin strained forward. It raced toward the reefs. The cold sea water flew into Ricky's face, but there wasn't time to wipe his eyes. He had to keep his hands on the wheel.

Ricky turned back to look at the other boat. It was right on his tail. And that was just where he wanted it to be. He would keep on moving fast.

The other boat would do the same. When the time was right, he would make a quick turn. He and the Marlin would be safe, but the other boat would hit the reefs.

The brown water was coming up fast. Suddenly a voice inside Ricky shouted: "NOW!" Ricky turned the wheel sharply, and the Marlin cut to the right. He heard a loud crash. He'd done it! He was safe. Or was he?

Just then he felt a hand grab his shoulder. Ricky screamed.

Jimmy, Tommy, and Ralph laughed.

"Hey," Tommy said, "what are you screaming about, Ricky?"

"Daydreaming again?" laughed Jimmy.

Ricky just stood there and stared.

Ralph pulled the captain's hat off Ricky's head. "I do believe Ricky has been playing captain again." Ralph tossed the hat to Jimmy.

Jimmy caught the hat and put it on his own head. "Hey, Ricky," he said, "that's a great job you have. Do you think Pulaski would pay me to play on this boat too?"

"I don't play. I work hard on this boat," said Ricky. He was starting to get angry.

Jimmy threw the hat back to Ralph. "Come off it, Ricky," said Ralph. "We know you spend all day fooling around. Admit it. You don't know the first thing about boats."

Ricky's face was getting hot. "I do too know

about boats!" he shouted. "And give me back that hat!"

"Come and get it!" Ralph laughed as he ran to the back of the boat. Jimmy and Tommy ran after him.

"Stop it!" shouted Ricky. "You can't run around on this boat! Please! You're going to get me in trouble! You've got to get off!"

CHAPTER 2

Ricky ran after his friends. When he got to the back of the Marlin, he looked around. Jimmy, Tommy, and Ralph were nowhere in sight.

"Hey, you guys!" Ricky shouted. "Where are you?"

No one answered. Ricky waited a moment and then tried again. "Come on, you guys. This isn't funny. Captain Pulaski is going to be back here any minute. If he catches you here, I'm finished."

Ralph and Tommy crawled out from their hiding places. They were laughing.

"Jimmy, come out!" Ricky yelled. "I'm not fooling around. Captain Pulaski will be furious if he finds you here. And, believe me, you don't want to get him mad."

"OK, OK," Jimmy called out. He crawled out from behind a big barrel. "Man, that Pulaski is mean," he said. "I'm glad I don't work for him."

"He's not mean," said Ricky. "He just doesn't like troublemakers on his boat."

"We're not troublemakers," said Ralph, grinning. "We just want to have a good time."

"Yeah, right," said Ricky. He looked up and down the dock to make sure Captain Pulaski

wasn't coming. "Look, the coast is clear now. You'd better go before he gets here."

"Not so fast," Jimmy said. "We 'troublemakers' will only leave on one condition."

"Name it," Ricky said. "And make it fast."

"We'll go now if you let us come back and hang out on the Marlin some night," said Jimmy.

"What?" said Ricky. "That's a joke, right?"

"No," Jimmy said. "We mean it. We were thinking that it would be kind of fun to hang out

on a boat for a change. What do you say?"

"No way!" said Ricky. "It's impossible!"

Tommy said, "Wait, Ricky, think about it. We could pretend that we were really at sea, going someplace exciting. You could be our captain, and we could be your crew. You could show us all the stuff Pulaski taught you. It would be fun."

Ricky looked up and down the dock again. He didn't see Captain Pulaski. "Look, you guys, your idea does sound like fun. But I can't do it."

"Why not?" asked Jimmy.

"I couldn't do that to Captain Pulaski," Ricky said. "He trusts me."

"Captain Pulaski, Captain Pulaski," Jimmy said. "That's all you ever talk about. You talk like he was the President or something."

"He's the best captain around," said Ricky. "And he's also my friend."

"What about us?" Ralph asked. "We're your friends too." He put the captain's hat on Ricky's head. "And we want to be your crew, Captain Ricky." Ralph turned to Jimmy and Tommy. "Isn't that right, guys?"

"Aye, aye!" they shouted.

"I'll think it over," said Ricky, "if you'll just go now. Please!"

Ralph, Tommy, and Jimmy went over to the boat's ladder.

"Don't forget," Jimmy called as they ran down the dock. "We'll be waiting for your answer."

"Well, don't hold your breath!" Ricky called back. He felt relieved to have them gone. He walked to the front of the boat. Without even thinking, he put his hands back on the wheel. He thought about what Tommy had said: "You could be our captain, and we could be your crew." Ricky had to admit, it really did sound like fun.

Just then Ricky heard his name called out. He looked over to the shore. Coming up the dock was Captain Pulaski.

"Oh, no," Ricky thought. "I hope he didn't see the guys." He put the captain's hat away, turned out the lights, and locked up. Then he dashed down the boat's ladder.

CHAPTER 3

Ricky raced down the dock. He didn't see Tommy, Jimmy, or Ralph anywhere. Just ahead Ricky could see Captain Pulaski. The captain waved.

"So you are here," the captain said. "I spotted lights aboard the Marlin, and I wondered what was going on. I figured you would be long gone by now."

"Oh, no," Ricky said. "I wouldn't leave the lights on. I always turn them off before I go home."

"Good," the captain said. He put his arm around Ricky's shoulders. "Now tell me something," he said. "What are you doing here so late? It's almost six o'clock. Did the Marlin need that much cleaning up?"

"Uh, no — not really," answered Ricky. "I was just . . ."

"It's OK," said the captain. "No need to explain. I can guess."

"Oh, no," Ricky thought. He hoped the captain couldn't guess — at least not about Tommy, Jimmy, and Ralph.

"What was it?" the captain asked. "A boat

race? Or was it pirates? I used to like pirates best."

Ricky was relieved. The captain must not have seen the guys after all. He was glad that he wouldn't have to lie. He *had* been pretending — at least until the guys showed up.

"A little of both," Ricky told the captain.

Captain Pulaski gave a deep laugh. "That's just what I thought. Is everything aboard the Marlin locked up?"

"Yes, sir," Ricky answered.

"Good. Then let's call it a night," said the captain. "It's getting late, and we sailors need our sleep."

"Right!" agreed Ricky. He looked over at the Marlin. "Good night, beauty," he whispered. Then he and Captain Pulaski walked off down the dock. Soon the ocean was behind them and they were on the city streets.

"Well," said the captain, "this is where I leave you, Ricky."

Ricky waved goodbye, and the captain turned a corner and disappeared down the street.

Ricky hurried up the block. "What a guy!" he thought. "He really understands what is what." But Ricky hadn't always thought that way. At first Ricky had been scared of Captain Pulaski. But now he knew better. Mostly the captain's bark was worse than his bite. If you were straight with him, he was straight with you. But if someone crossed him — well, that was something else. He was not a guy you wanted mad at you.

Ricky turned the corner at Wilson's Candy Store. He stopped short. Inside he spotted Jimmy, Tommy, and Ralph.

"Oh no!" Ricky said to himself. He didn't want them to see him. Quickly he ducked past the store window. Then he began to run. After a

while he stopped running and looked back.

"That was close," he said to himself. He went on more slowly. A few more blocks and he would be home.

As Ricky walked, he thought about the guys. They were his friends, but sometimes they could be bad news. Why were they bugging him about sneaking them on board? Didn't they realize that he would probably lose his job if they got caught playing around on the Marlin? Of course, they could have a lot of fun if they didn't get caught. They had said he could be the captain, and they would be his crew. It would sure be fun bossing them around for a change. And he could show them a thing or two: like how to read the waters.

"What am I thinking of!?" Ricky said out loud.

"What are you thinking of?" asked Ricky's mother. "You've been standing at this door, completely still, for five minutes."

"Oh, hi, Mom," Ricky said. "I was just thinking about the Marlin."

Ricky's mother laughed. "Somehow that doesn't surprise me. How would it be if you continued your thinking inside, while you set the table for dinner?" She opened the door wide.

Ricky grinned at his mother and stepped inside. "I could be the captain, and they could be my crew," he thought as he set the table. "Maybe it's not so impossible!"

CHAPTER 4

Early the next day Ricky was on board the Marlin. He had a lot to do. The fishing rods had to be taken out. The bait pails had to be filled. And then he had to fix lunch for himself and the captain. Everything had to be done by 6:00 a.m. That was when the passengers would start coming aboard.

"Well, Ricky," said the captain, "how is the work coming?"

"Fine, Captain," Ricky answered. "I'm almost finished."

The summer sun appeared over the dock. Soon it was time, and the passengers started arriving. Ricky stood by the ladder and helped them climb aboard.

There were lots of families sailing today. Ricky was glad. Family days on the Marlin were always a lot of fun. The Marlin could hold 20 people, and it was almost full.

"All right, Ricky," called Captain Pulaski, "it's 6:30, and we're ready to shove off now. Raise the ladder."

"Wait!" Ricky called back. "There's still someone coming."

Someone was running up the dock. Ricky could see it was Jimmy.

"Jimmy!" Ricky said. "What are you doing here?"

"I'm going fishing," Jimmy said. "Same as everyone else. My uncle invited me to go."

"Then where is he?" asked Ricky.

"On the boat," Jimmy said. "I waited until I would be the last one on board so that I could surprise you. Surprise!"

"Ricky!" the captain called again. "What is holding us up? Clear the ladder away."

"Yes, sir!" Ricky called. He turned to Jimmy. "Listen, Jimmy. I have work to do. I'll catch you later."

"Sure," Jimmy said. "No problem."

The Marlin's engines began to roar. Just in time, Ricky pulled up the ladder. Now they were really moving. What a day! And having Jimmy aboard would make the day even more satisfying for Ricky. Jimmy was always teasing him about daydreaming and goofing off. But today Ricky would show him a few things. Jimmy would see that Ricky knew what he was doing on the Marlin.

"Ricky," called the captain, "I need you over here."

Ricky hurried over to the wheel. "Yes, sir."

"I'm afraid we're going to have to head back in. Our trip is over for today," the captain said.

"Over!?" Ricky asked. "How can it be over? We haven't even left the harbor!"

"I know," said the captain, "but there is a storm warning out. I just got it over the radio. It may blow over. But then again it may not. A storm can come up fast. We can't take a chance."

"I don't believe this," Ricky thought. "Just when everything was going so well."

"Tell the passengers," the captain said. "Tell them that we will return their money."

Ricky walked off. He told one passenger, then another, and another. After that the news traveled all by itself. Soon everyone on board knew why they were headed back.

Ricky pulled out the boat's ladder. Then he went to look for Jimmy. But it was Jimmy who found him.

"Pulaski must be kidding!" Jimmy said. "There isn't a cloud in the sky. There is no reason to turn back!"

"What do you know about it?" asked Ricky. "If Captain Pulaski says there will be a storm, there will be."

"Yeah, when?" asked Jimmy. "Three weeks from now?"

"You don't know anything," Ricky said. "Storms can come up fast. You can't take chances with people's lives. Any good captain knows that. Captain Pulaski knows exactly what he's doing."

"How would you know?" Jimmy sneered. "You don't know anything about boats."

"I do too!" Ricky said loudly. "I know a lot!"

"Oh yeah?" Jimmy said. "Prove it. I bet you can't."

"I can too!" Ricky said.

"OK," said Jimmy. "Then let me and the guys hang out on the Marlin tonight. We'll see for ourselves whether you know anything about boats."

24

Ricky swallowed hard. "Uh, tonight?"

"Yeah, tonight," said Jimmy. "We'll be at the dock at five o'clock. You'll be there too, right?"

"Uh, yeah . . . sure," Ricky said. He hoped he didn't sound as worried as he felt.

CHAPTER 5

The Marlin slowly pulled in to dock. Ricky helped the captain tie up the boat. Then he went into the cabin below. He didn't say goodbye to the passengers as he usually did. He didn't want to see Jimmy again. Jimmy had really made him angry.

"I lost my cool," Ricky said to himself. "How could I have agreed to let those guys come onto the Marlin tonight? I must be nuts!"

"Ricky, come up here," he heard the captain call. "I have to talk to you."

"Oh, no," Ricky thought. "What if he knows? What if Jimmy told him something?" Ricky rushed up top.

"Here I am," he said. "Is everything OK?"

"Well, of course," Captain Pulaski said. "I just wanted us to get started. I have a plan for the rest of the day."

"Oh," Ricky said. He let out his breath.

"We're going to paint the cabin," the captain said. "Now is the perfect time."

Ricky went and got two brushes. Captain Pulaski took out the paint. They set to work.

Ricky didn't talk much. He was jumpy, too.

After a while Captain Pulaski gave him a worried look.

"Are you all right?" he asked.

"I'm fine," Ricky answered.

"If something is wrong," the captain said, "we could talk about it. It might make you feel better."

Ricky thought it over for a second. Part of him wanted to tell the captain everything. But another part said no.

"It's nothing," Ricky finally said. "I guess I'm just disappointed. Here we are at shore, and that storm never even came."

"Not yet," said the captain. "But it still might. You never know with storms in these parts. Sometimes they surprise you."

At last the cabin was all painted. Captain Pulaski looked at the ship's clock. "It's 4:30 already!" he said. "I was supposed to be home fifteen minutes ago. Ricky, I hate to do this to you, but I'm going to have to leave."

"That's OK, Captain Pulaski," Ricky said. "I'll take care of cleaning up."

"Do you remember how to clean the brushes?" asked the captain.

"Yes, sir," said Ricky.

"That's my boy. I can always count on you, Ricky," the captain said. "Now, I'd better be going." Captain Pulaski waved goodbye. Then he hurried off the boat.

Ricky started cleaning up. He felt awful. The captain had said, "I can always count on you, Ricky." What a joke! Ricky knew that it wasn't true anymore. Not since he had agreed to let Jimmy and the other guys come on board the Marlin. He wished he hadn't said those things to Jimmy. He wished that Jimmy hadn't come on the boat at all that day. He wished a lot of things, but it was no use. His three friends would be on the boat soon, and there was nothing he could do about it.

Ricky put away the brushes and the leftover paint. Suddenly he had an idea. "I could leave before they showed up," he thought. "I could leave right now." He started out the cabin door, but then he stopped himself.

"That's no good. If I leave now, the guys will think I'm chicken." He looked at the clock. "Where are they? It's after five o'clock." Then he thought: "Hey, maybe they chickened out!" Ricky grabbed his things and went up top. But when he got there, he saw his three friends. Jimmy, Tommy, and Ralph were just climbing aboard the Marlin.

Jimmy was the first one up. "Hey, Ricky," he said, "that was some storm we had today, wasn't it? I was telling the guys here that there was so much water everywhere that the boat almost sank. It was lucky for us that Captain Pulaski got us back to shore before we drowned!"

Tommy and Ralph didn't seem to know what Jimmy was talking about. They just looked at each other and shrugged their shoulders.

"That's very funny, Jimmy," Ricky said. "Now listen, you guys, we just finished painting the cabin. The paint is wet, so be careful not to touch it, OK?"

"Aye, aye, Captain!" Jimmy shouted. Tommy and Ralph chuckled.

Ricky was thinking of what else he should tell the guys about the Marlin. But Jimmy didn't wait to hear. He pushed past Ricky, grabbing Tommy and Ralph.

"Let's go, you guys!" Jimmy shouted. "It's time to have some fun." They made their way to the back of the boat. Ricky couldn't see what they were doing.

"Hey, wait a minute!" Ricky yelled. "Come back here!"

Jimmy turned around. "What's the problem?" he asked.

"I don't want you guys just running around," Ricky said. "You said that I could be captain and you would be my crew. That means you have to take orders from me."

Jimmy looked at Tommy and Ralph. "What do you think, guys, should we let him be our captain?"

Ralph said, "I don't know, what do you think, Tommy?"

Ricky broke in, "Hey, this isn't fair. You promised I could be captain. We made a deal, remember?"

Jimmy said, "Oh, all right. But you better not make us swab the deck or anything. We want to have some fun, right, guys?" Jimmy looked at Tommy and Ralph.

"Right!" they shouted. The three boys started to laugh.

"OK, crew," Ricky said. "Here's what we're going to do." The boys quieted down. "We're going to pretend we are really at sea. Each of you will have a job to do. Jimmy, you will be my first mate. You can take the wheel and steer the boat for me for a while. Ralph, you can be the navigator. Your job is to study the charts and figure out how to get where we are going. And Tommy, you can be the look-out man. You can use the telescope to watch for pirates or enemy ships. Do you all understand what you're supposed to do?"

"Aye, aye, Captain," they answered. Then the boys split up and went to do their jobs. Ricky was surprised. "They actually took orders from me," he said to himself. He felt proud for a moment. "They're not such bad guys," he thought. "They just want to have some fun, and there's nothing wrong with that. Or is there?" he wondered.

CHAPTER 6

"Take that, you worm!" shouted Ricky. He held a mop handle out like a sword. On his head was the captain's hat. He was fighting with make-believe pirates.

"Throw them overboard," yelled Ralph.

"Feed them to the sharks," yelled Tommy.

"Tie them to these ropes," yelled Jimmy. "And leave them — "

"Time out," called Ricky. "Stay away from the ropes. Don't touch any of them."

"I didn't touch them," said Jimmy. "I was just pointing."

"OK," said Ricky. Then he shouted, "The plank! The plank! We should make them all walk the plank." Then, one by one, they pushed the pirates off into the water.

"That takes care of that," Ricky said with a laugh.

"Yeah," agreed Ralph. "But am I thirsty now!"

"Me, too," Jimmy said. "And I'm getting hungry. Is there anything to drink or eat around this place?"

"There should be," said Ricky. "Come down below. I'll take a look. But be careful not to

touch the wet paint." Ricky began to climb down into the cabin. Ralph and Jimmy followed him.

"Hey, Tommy, aren't you coming down?" Ricky asked.

"I'm not thirsty," Tommy said. "I'll wait up here."

Below, the boys found a bottle of milk. They also found bread, butter, and jam. "This is great," Ralph said, in between swallows.

"Yeah," said Jimmy, "but leave some for us!"

Just then Tommy called down. "Hey, Ricky. What are those ropes for anyway?" he asked.

"What ropes?" asked Ricky. "I can't see what you mean from down here."

"You know," answered Tommy. "The two ropes you told us not to touch. One was in the front of the boat, and the other was in the back."

"What do you mean *was?*" said Ricky. "Aren't they still there?"

"Well, they're still there, but they're not in the boat," Tommy said. "They're in the water."

"That's impossible!" cried Ricky. "Those ropes hold the boat to the dock. They are tied in two places, front and back. If they weren't, we would be drifting out to sea by now."

"Ricky," said Tommy, "I think we *are* drifting out to sea."

"What!" screamed Ricky. He was up top in a flash. Jimmy and Ralph ran after him. First Ricky dashed to the back of the boat. Then he ran up front. But it was too late. Tommy was right. Somehow the ropes had come undone, and the Marlin was drifting out into the harbor.

"Oh, no," cried Ricky. "It's all over! Now we're finished!"

Jimmy, Tommy, and Ralph didn't say a word. They just stood and stared.

"All right!" yelled Ricky. "Which one of you did this?"

"None of us did," said Ralph.

"That's not true!" Ricky yelled. "It must have been you, Tommy."

"I never touched the ropes! Never!" cried Tommy.

"Well, somebody did," Ricky said. "They couldn't have come loose on their own."

"They must have," said Jimmy. "None of us touched those ropes! Maybe they came undone while we were playing. But who cares? Right now you've got to do something. You've got to get us back."

Ralph said, "Yeah, you're the big shot who knows so much about boats. At least you said you did."

"Do something!" cried Tommy. "We could get lost at sea."

"All right, all right," said Ricky. "Just be quiet for a minute. Give me a chance to think."

"Then think fast!" said Ralph. "It's getting dark, and this boat is not exactly standing still."

Ricky looked at the dock. It was too far away for him to swim back. "What would Captain Pulaski do right now?" he wondered. "He would kill me! That's what he would do! Why did I ever let these guys on board?"

Then Ricky had an idea. "My keys!" he said. "Maybe one of them will start the boat. Then I can drive us back to shore!"

"OK," said Ralph. "That's what I call thinking."

"Our worries are over!" shouted Tommy.

Ricky ran over to the Marlin's wheel. The

others followed close behind.

"Boy," Ricky thought to himself. "I hope I know what I'm doing. This looks harder than I thought."

Just then Tommy began tugging at Ricky's arm. "Hey, did you feel that?" he said.

"Did I feel what?" asked Ricky.

"The rain!" Tommy said. "You'd better get us back fast. It's beginning to rain."

CHAPTER 7

The Marlin was still drifting out into the harbor. It had started to rain. It was getting dark fast, and wind rocked the boat. Tommy was beginning to feel sick.

"What's taking so long, Ricky?" asked Jimmy. "I thought you said you knew about all these things."

Ricky glared at Jimmy. "I do," he said. "I just can't find the right key. None of these will fit the starter."

"One of them has to," said Jimmy. "Here, hand them over. I'll do it." Jimmy tried to grab the keys.

"Let go!" yelled Ricky. "Get your hands off them!" He lunged at Jimmy and pushed him out of the way.

"Hey, what's your problem?" said Jimmy. "I was just trying to help."

"I'll tell you how you can help me," said Ricky. "Leave me alone!"

"Why should we leave you alone?" said Ralph. "We're stuck in the middle of the ocean. It's dark. It's raining. I'm getting wet. And Captain Ricky can't do a thing!"

"Shut up, Ralph," said Ricky. He was really getting mad.

"I don't feel so good," said Tommy. "I think I'm going to be sick."

"Oh, no," said Ralph. "That's all we need. Just don't get sick near me."

"Yeah," said Jimmy. "Lean over the side, away from the wind!"

"Hold on, everybody!" cried Ricky. "I found it! I found the right key!"

"It took you long enough," grumbled Jimmy. "Don't just stand there, start the boat!"

Ricky made a face at Jimmy. Then he said, "Here goes!" Ralph pushed in closer to watch. Ricky turned the key, and the engine started with a roar.

"What's this stick for?" asked Ralph. He was looking at the stick next to the wheel.

"It's called the throttle," Ricky said. "It's like a gas pedal on a car. If you push it forward, it makes the boat go faster."

Ralph reached out to touch it.

"Stop!" Ricky said. "Don't do that! The boat's engine is on!" But Ralph wasn't listening. Ricky tried to grab Ralph's hand off the throttle, but Ralph pushed down harder. He didn't let go. And then it happened. The Marlin shot straight out into the harbor.

"Stop the boat!" screamed Tommy. "Please! Do something!"

"I can't," Ricky said. "The throttle is stuck! It won't move!"

"Turn off the engine!" Jimmy yelled.

"I'm afraid to!" said Ricky. "If I turn it off now, it might not start up again."

"Look what you've done, Ralph!" Jimmy shouted. "Why did you have to play around with the throttle? That was a stupid thing to do. You only made things worse!"

"I was trying to see how it worked," Ralph said. "How was I supposed to know it would get stuck?"

"Everybody, be quiet!" yelled Ricky. He was trying to concentrate. The boat was moving fast, and the rain was coming down harder now. Ricky held tightly to the wheel. He had to keep the Marlin straight. It was the only thing he could do.

Ricky thought back to that morning. It seemed like a very long time ago now. "If only I hadn't let those guys push me around!" he said to himself. "If only I hadn't let them on the boat, none of this would have happened."

Jimmy came over and tried to fix the throttle. He pushed and pulled at it. But it was no use. The throttle just wouldn't budge.

Suddenly they heard a moan. It was Tommy. He was hanging over the side of the boat. Now he was really sick!

"Tommy! Grab onto that pole!" yelled Jimmy.

"You are going to fall!"

"I — I can't. I can't reach it," cried Tommy.

"Help him," Ricky said to Jimmy. "I can't leave the wheel." Jimmy ran over to Tommy's side.

Suddenly Ralph began to scream. "Look!" he cried, pointing. "Look! We are moving out of the harbor!"

Ricky looked. Ralph was right. Now there was nothing but the open sea ahead of them.

CHAPTER 8

The Marlin was still moving quickly through the water. The boys looked back. They could no longer see the shore.

The rain was still coming down, but the boys hardly noticed. The rain was the least of their worries. All their thoughts were on turning the boat around. They wanted to go home.

"Do something, Ricky," shouted Ralph. "We're going out too far. We'll never get back."

Ricky gave Ralph a mean look. "I wouldn't say anything if I were you, Ralph. It's your fault that the throttle is stuck, remember?"

Ralph didn't answer. He just looked away.

"Jimmy, why don't you take the wheel and let me work on the throttle?" said Ricky.

Jimmy shrugged his shoulders. "Be my guest," he said. Then he took over at the wheel. Ricky grabbed the throttle with both hands. It was still stuck, but this time he was not going to give up. He had to keep trying. He pulled at it with all his might.

"I think it moved!" Ricky yelled. He took a deep breath. Again and again he pulled at the throttle, until at last it came unstuck and jerked

back into place. But then the engine stalled. The Marlin slowed to a stop. Now that the engine was off, it was very quiet. All they could hear was the sound of the rain.

"Well," said Ricky, "I fixed the throttle."

"Yeah," said Jimmy. "And you stalled the engine. Now what are we going to do? How are we going to get back to — "

"Hey," Ralph said. "Where's Tommy?"

The boys looked around. "You saw him last, Jimmy," said Ricky. "Where was he?"

"Right there," said Jimmy. He pointed out the spot. "He was hanging onto that pole. He was kind of leaning over the side and — "

"Oh, no!" Ricky yelled. "He fell into the water!

He might be drowning!"

"Tommy! Tommy!" the boys screamed. "Where are you?" They stared into the dark water. Then they heard Tommy's voice. It sounded far away.

"Please, you guys!" cried Tommy. "You've got to stop yelling. I'm sick. I feel sick!"

"Wait a minute," Ricky said. "You're supposed to be drowning!"

"Drowning? Who's drowning?" they heard Tommy call.

Just then Jimmy figured out what was happening. "Ricky, Ralph!" he said. "Tommy isn't in the water. He's down in the cabin!" Quickly they ran down below.

"We thought you were overboard!" said Ralph.

"Yeah," said Jimmy. "You had us scared. We thought you were done for!"

"I am done for," said Tommy. "I'm sick!"

"But why did you come down here?" asked Ricky.

"I thought being inside would help," Tommy answered. "But so far it hasn't."

"Well, I know something that might help," said Ricky. "I think I know a way to get us home fast."

"What's your bright idea this time?" said Jimmy.

"Look, do you want to know it or don't you?" said Ricky. Jimmy was really getting on his nerves.

"Let's hear it," said Jimmy.

"Well, every boat has a radio — " Ricky began.

"Oh, yeah," said Jimmy, "and we're going to use it to call for help, is that it?"

"Got any better ideas?" said Ricky.

"Not at the moment. Where is the radio?" said Jimmy.

"It's upstairs," said Ricky. "Come on."

The boys followed Ricky upstairs to the boat's radio. Ricky turned all the dials. At last it came on. They tried talking into it, but it was no good. Nothing happened. No one seemed to hear them.

"Don't you know how to work this thing?" Ralph asked Ricky.

"Well, not exactly," admitted Ricky. "I've seen Captain Pulaski use it, but I've never had to use it myself." He turned the dials around again. For a while all they heard was noises. Then a voice came on. The boys listened. Then all at once they became frightened — more frightened than before. The voice said one thing over and over: "STORM WARNING! STORM WARNING!"

The boys looked at each other. Suddenly they heard a clap of thunder. Then the radio went dead.

CHAPTER 9

Lightning streaked across the sky. Strong winds rocked the boat. And angry waves began to beat against the sides. Thunder boomed out, loud as gunshots. Ricky's three friends began to panic.

"Help!" screamed Ralph. "We're going to get killed! We're going to die out here!"

"Stop it!" yelled Ricky. "You're making me nervous. Please, just get down in the cabin. All of you."

"But what are you going to do?" asked Jimmy.

"I don't know yet, but I'll think of something," said Ricky. "Now please go downstairs."

Jimmy, Tommy, and Ralph started for the cabin. It was hard not to fall. The storm was making the boat pitch and roll.

"Good," Ricky said to himself. "Now that they're out of my hair I'll be able to think." He closed his eyes. He could almost see Captain Pulaski. "If only I could somehow get him here," he thought, "then we would be saved. He would know what to do."

But thinking that way was no good. It wouldn't get them home.

Ricky opened his eyes. "What is going on?" he said. Jimmy, Tommy, and Ralph were standing there, staring at him. "How long have you guys been here?"

"Only a second or two," said Jimmy. "We couldn't stay down there in the cabin. It smells like paint in there. It was making us all feel sick."

Ricky stood facing the other boys. Rain dripped down everyone's face. "Listen," Ricky said. "The boat can't take much more of this. And neither can we. I'm going to try driving us in again."

Ricky grabbed the wheel. This time he found the right key without any trouble. He put the key into the starter and slowly turned it. At once the engine began to roar. Then Ricky carefully moved the throttle forward.

"This is it!" he yelled. The Marlin jumped out fast. Heavy waves banged against the boat. The rain came down in sheets. It was worse than ever.

The first thing Ricky had to do was turn the boat around. But the water was so rough that moving the wheel was a real fight. He turned the wheel with all his might, until at last the Marlin came around. For a moment the rain cleared, and Ricky could just make out the shore. He had done it! They were headed toward the harbor.

"Just keep the boat straight," he told himself.
"That's all I have to do now."

Twice Ricky almost lost control of the wheel.
The deck was wet and slippery. It was hard to
stay on his feet.

"Come on," he whispered. "We can do it. I
know we can."

Ricky could make out the docks up ahead. It had been a close fight, but they were going to win. He and the Marlin were going to save the day! Ricky felt great as he pushed forward on the throttle.

Just then Jimmy grabbed Ricky's arm. "What are you doing!" he yelled. "Slow down! We're going to hit the dock!"

Ricky hadn't been watching carefully. He had

been too busy daydreaming about saving the day. He reached for the throttle and yanked it back. But it was too late. They would never stop in time.

"Hit the deck!" Ricky yelled. "Hit the deck, everybody! We are going to — "

Ricky never had a chance to finish. The Marlin crashed into the dock and stopped. Their ride was over.

CHAPTER 10

Ricky slowly got up. He took a look at his friends. No one was hurt. Then he looked around the Marlin. The first thing he looked at was the clock. Its glass was broken, but it was still running.

"It's eight o'clock! We were out there for three hours," Ricky said.

That made Tommy, Jimmy, and Ralph jump up fast.

"It's really late!" Jimmy said. "Let's get out of here."

"Yeah," agreed Tommy. "I'm sick of boats."

"Hold on!" said Ricky. "We can't leave yet. The Marlin hit the dock pretty hard. It's probably in bad shape. We'd better find out how bad."

Ricky and the others climbed down onto the dock and began to look the Marlin over.

"Oh, no!" Ricky said. "Look at this. The paint is all scratched off the side!"

"Oh, well," Ralph said. "It can always be painted again."

"Yeah," said Jimmy. "Scratched-off paint is no big deal."

Ricky thought it was a big deal, but he didn't

59

say anything. He just walked to the front of the boat.

"Oh, no!" he said. "Look at that!" He pointed toward a big dent.

"That is bad," Tommy said.

"Don't I know it!" Ricky said. "Fixing this

could cost hundreds of dollars! Where are we going to get that kind of money?"

"We?" yelled Ralph. "Are you nuts? We don't even have five dollars between us!"

"Look, I say we get out of here," Jimmy said. "And the sooner, the better. If anyone catches us here, we're through."

"What are you talking about?" asked Ricky.

"I'm talking about saving our skins," Jimmy answered.

"Right," said Tommy. "Pulaski would kill us if he found out about tonight."

"But he has to find out," said Ricky. "It's no use. He will see the Marlin tomorrow. Then he will know everything."

"Maybe not," said Jimmy. "So far no one has seen us. If we leave now, no one will. And don't forget, everyone knows about the storm."

"What are you trying to say?" Ricky asked.

"I'm saying," Jimmy answered, "that Pulaski never has to know about us. Let him blame the storm. It won't be a lie. The storm really did dent the boat."

"Yeah," Ricky said, "but — "

"But nothing," Ralph said. "Let him think it all happened while the Marlin was tied up at the dock."

"How it really happened doesn't matter," Tommy said. "Why should we get in trouble? Let's just go."

"Wait," Ricky said. "I need time to think."

"Look, Ricky. We've already made up our minds," said Jimmy. "We're going to go." Jimmy, Tommy, and Ralph began slowly walking away.

Ricky sat down on the dock. "Maybe they're right," he thought to himself. "The truth would make the captain angry. I broke his rules. I should never have let the guys aboard. I'll probably get fired."

"Come on, Ricky. Don't be a dope," called Jimmy. He and the other boys had turned around to see what Ricky was doing.

Ricky wasn't listening. "I sure don't want to lose my job," he thought, "but I can't lie to Captain Pulaski. He's my friend, and he deserves to know the truth."

Ricky slowly got up from the dock and started to walk off.

"Hey, where are you going?" shouted Jimmy. "We're over here. Home is this way."

"I'm not going home," Ricky answered. "I'm going to see Captain Pulaski."

"What! Are you crazy?" shouted Ralph.

"No," said Ricky. "Protecting the Marlin was

my job, and I blew it. I have to tell the truth. It's important."

"Well, leave us out of it," Jimmy said.

"Don't worry," said Ricky. "I'll tell him that it was all my fault. Why don't you guys just go on home."

Jimmy, Tommy, and Ralph started walking again. Then Jimmy turned around one more time. "Don't say we didn't warn you," he said.

Ricky didn't answer. Instead he turned to look at the Marlin — maybe for the last time. Then he turned toward Captain Pulaski's house. He took a deep breath. Then he began to run.